The Adventures of Ulysses the Wanderer

Retold by C. Ranger-Gull

NATAL PUBLISHING LLC

ARS LONGA, VITA BREVIS

The
THE FIRST EPISODE

How They blinded the Son of Poseidon

A warm mild wind, laden with sweet scents, blew over the sailors from the island, which now lay far astern.

In the weary west the charmed sunset still lingered over Lotus Land.

A rosy flush lay on the snow-capped mountains which were yet spectral in the last lights of the day, but looking out over the bows the sky was dark purple changing into black, and where it met the sea there was a white gleam of foam.

The companions of Ulysses sat idle from the oars, for the wind filled the belly of the sail and there was no need for rowing. A curious silence brooded over them all. No one spoke to his fellow. The faces of all were sad, and in the eyes of some the fire of an unutterable regret burnt steadily.

The heads of all were turned towards the island, which was fast disappearing from their view. Some of the men shaded their eyes with their hands in one last long look of farewell.

As the curtain of the dark fell upon the sea, the warm offshore wind died away. A colder breeze,

full of the sea-smell itself, came down over the port bow; it moaned through the cordage, and little waves began to hiss under the cutwater.

Every now and again the wind freshened rapidly. The mournful whistling became a sudden snarling of trumpets. The ship and crew seemed to have passed over the limits of a tableau. Not only was it a quick elemental change of scene, but the change had its influence with the spectators.

The sad fire—if the glow of regret is indeed a fire—died out of heavy eyes half veiled by weary lids. The sea-light dawned once more upon the faces of the mariners, the bright warm blood moved swiftly in their veins.

One man ran to the steering oar to give an aid to the helmsman as the ship went about on the starboard tack, three more stood by the sheet, a hum of talk rose from the waist of the boat. Ulysses stood in the bows looking forward into the night. His tall, lean figure was bent forward, and his arm was thrown round the gilded boss of the prow. His eyes were deep set in his head, and his brow was furrowed with the innumerable wrinkles which come to the man who lives a life of hardship and striving.

Yet the long years of battle and wandering, a life of shocks! had only intensified the alertness of his pose. He seemed, as he looked out into the night, a personification of "readiness." A crisp dark beard grew round his throat, and the veins on his bare brown arms were like blue enamel round a column of bronze.

When the ship went about again he came down into the body of the ship and helped to pull upon the brace. Though he was no taller than many of his men, and leaner than most, in physical strength as well as in intellect he was first and chief. The mighty muscles leapt up on his arms as he strained on the taut rope.

The ship slanted away down the wind into the night. The men gathered round their captain. "Comrades," he said to them in a singularly sweet and musical voice, "once more we adventure the deep, and no man knows what shall befall us. To our island home in the west, to dear Ithaca! if the gods so will it. Our wives weep for us on our deserted hearthstone. Our little ones are noble youths ere now, and may Zeus bring us safe home at last. Yet much it misdoubts me that there are other perils in store for us ere we hear the long breakers beat upon the shores of Ithaca and see the morning sun run down the wooded sides of Neriton. Be that as the Fates will it, let us keep always courage, gaiety, and the quiet mind."

"We are well away from there," said one of the men, nodding vaguely towards the stern.

"That are we," said another; "that cursed fruit is honeysweet in my mouth still. It stole away our brains and made us as women, we! the men who fought in Troyland."

"Of what profit is it to look to the past, Phocion?" said Ulysses. "We did eat and sleep and forget, but it is over. The sea wind is salt once more upon our faces. Let us eat the night meal, and then I will choose a watch and the rest may sleep. Hand me the cup—To to-morrow's dawn!"

Then one of the sailors took dried goat's flesh and fruit from a locker in the stern, and by the light of a torch of sawn sandal wood they fell to eating. Great bunches of purple grapes lay before each sailor, but they had brought none of the magic lotus fruit with them to steal away their vigour and thicken their blood.

Then they lay down to sleep under coverings of skins. Two men went to the great steering oar, three men watched amidship by the braces, and Ulysses himself wrapped a woollen cloak round him and went once more into the bows.

Alone there with the wind his thoughts once more went back to his far distant home. He thought with longing of his old father Laertes, of the child Telemachus playing in the marble courtyard of the sunny palace on the hill. A deep sigh shuddered out from his lips as his thoughts fell upon the lonely Queen Penelope. "Wife of mine," he thought, "shall I ever lie beside you more? Is there silver in your bright hair now? Are your thoughts to mewards as mine to you? Perchance another rules in my palace and sits at my seat. Are your lips another's now? The great tears are blinding me. Courage!"

Bending his head upon his breast, Ulysses prayed long and earnestly to his awful patroness, the Goddess Athene, that she would still keep ward over his fortunes and guide him safely home.

The night wore on and became very silent. The ship seemed to be moving swiftly and surely, though the wind had dropped and the voice of the waves was hushed. It seemed to the watcher in the bows that the ship was moving in the path of some strong current.

A curious white mist suddenly rolled over the still surface of the sea, thick and ghostly. The mast and sail, which was now drooping and lifeless, swayed through it like giant spectres. Ulysses could see none of his companions, but when he hailed the watch the voice of Phocion came back to him through the ghostly curtain, curiously thick and muffled.

"The mist thickens, my captain," said the sailor. "Can you see aught ahead?"

"I can see nothing, Phocion," shouted Ulysses; "the mist is like wool. But I think it is a land mist come out to meet us. There should be land ahead."

"I hear no surf or the rolling of waves," said Phocion. "May Zeus guide the boat, for mortal men are of no avail to-night."

The ship moved on swiftly as if guided by invisible hands towards some goal, and still the expectant mariners heard no sound.

Quite suddenly, and without the slightest warning, a vivid copper-coloured flash of lightning illuminated the ship. For an instant in the hard lurid light Ulysses saw the whole of the vessel in a distinct picture.

Every detail was manifest—the mast, the cordage,

the sleeping sailors below, the watching group by the shrouds, and, right away astern, the startled helmsmen motionless as statues of bronze.

Then with a long grinding noise the ship seemed suddenly lifted up in the water, jerked forward, and then dropped again. She began to heel over a little out of the perpendicular, and then remained still, stranded upon an unknown and mysterious shore, where the waves were all asleep. Still the white mist circled round them.

"Comrades," said Ulysses, "we are brought here by no chance of wind and waves. Some god has done this thing, but whether for weal or woe I cannot tell. Let us land upon the beach and lie down with our weapons within sound of the sea till dawn. At sunrise we shall know where the god has brought us."

They landed at the order, and with the supreme indifference of the adventurer lay upon the shore and slept out the remainder of the night. But Ulysses had a prescience of harm, and was full of sinister forebodings. He did not sleep, but paced through the mist all night in a little beaten track among the boulders. He prayed long and earnestly to Athene.

When the first faint hintings of dawn brightened through the mist a little breeze arose, and before the sky was more than faintly flushed with day the night fog was blown away like thistledown.

As the sun climbed up the sky the companions found that they had been carried to a scene of

singular beauty. They were on an island, a small, rich place at the mouth of a great bay. Rich level grass meadows, green as bright enamel and brilliant with flowers, sloped gently down to the violet sea. Behind was a thickly-wooded hill, at the foot of which was a sparkling spring surrounded by a tall grove of poplar trees.

In the leafy wood the wild goats leapt under the wild vine trees like Pan at play, as fearless of the intruders as if they had never seen men before. All the bright morning the sailors made the wood ring with happy laughter as they speared the goats for a feast. All trouble passed from their minds, and as the spears flashed swiftly through the green wood the shrill, jocund voices of the hunters made all the island musical. Ulysses plunged into a translucent pool at the foot of the spring, and the cool water flashed like diamonds over his strong brown arms, and he looked indeed as if he were some river-god and this his fairy home.

All day long they feasted and drank wine which they had brought in skins from Lotus Land. When night was falling, very still and gentle, they saw the blue smoke of fires over the bay, on the mainland, about a mile away, and the bleating of many sheep and the lowing of herds came to them over the wine-coloured sea.

Ever and again voices could be heard—strange resonant voices. "That must be the country of some strange gods," the sailors said to each other. "Those are no mortal voices. We are come into some great peril." Before they slept they sacrificed

a goat on the seashore to Zeus, that he might guard them from any coming harm.

In the morning the king prepared for action. It was necessary to find upon what shores they had arrived, to get direction of Ithaca, and if treasure was to be won by force or guile, to take the opportunity which chance or the gods had sent.

Ulysses chose twelve of his men, tried veterans with nerves of steel, old comrades who had fought with him for Helen on the windy plains of Troy. With these old never-strikes he embarked on the ship. He left Phocion as leader of the remainder of the crew, and taking Elpenor with him as second in command, they got out six sweeps, three on each side of the ship, and rowed slowly over the glassy bay.

The mainland, on the shore where they landed, was a wild rocky place, and there was a broad road winding away up to the higher pasture lands. The road was made of great rocks beaten into smoothness, and fresh spoor of cattle showed that not long since a great herd had passed to the upland feeding grounds.

Directly in front of them as they landed was a high cave. It was fringed with laurel bushes, which grew on ledges in the cliff side.

Before the cave a great wall had been built in a square, forming a courtyard. The wall was built with enormous masses of rock, and fenced with a palisade of pine trunks and massive boles of oak. There was no sign of any living thing. Slowly

and cautiously the party crept up to the wall. Their weapons were in readiness as they stole through the gateway. Within the square formed by the wall they could see that it was a vast cattle pen. "This must be the dwelling of some giant," said Elpenor; "men do not build like this. On what strange place have we chanced?" He looked inquiringly at Ulysses when he had spoken, and a ring of eager faces turned towards him whose wisdom was never at fault, the favourite of Athene.

"I think, comrades," said Ulysses, "that we have been driven to the shores of the Cyclopes. They are mighty giants, who work in the forge of Vulcan making armour for the gods. Now this cave must be the dwelling of one of them, and I like not where we are. Let us but go within for a short time and take what we can find, and then hasten back to the island. The Cyclopes have no boats and cannot follow us. But it would go hard with us were we found, for they are crafty and cruel monsters."

With hasty, curious footsteps they crossed the echoing flags of the courtyard and entered the cave. As the shadow of the entrance fell upon them and the chill of the air inside struck on their faces, more than one would have gladly stayed in the warm outside sunshine. It was an ill-omened, sinister place this lair of giants.

A pungent ammoniacal smell made them cough and shudder as they crossed the threshold. Ulysses turned with a grim smile to his followers.

"Thank the gods we are seamen and sons of the fresh wind. This Cyclops lives like a swine in a stye." The large entrance to the cave gave a fair light within, and their eyes soon became accustomed to it. Along one side of the cave were folds of fat lambs and kids who bleated lustily at them. At the end of the cave was a great couch of skins by the ashes of a pine fire. Bones and scraps of flesh were piled round, relics of some great orgy, and a sickly stench of decay came from the *débris*.

Piles of wicker baskets were loaded with huge yellow cheeses, and there were many copper milk pails and bowls brimful of whey.

The sailors rejoiced at such an abundance of good cheer, and they killed one of the fattest of the lambs and lit a fire to roast it.

"The giant will not return till even," said Elpenor, "and by then we shall be far away. We will make a good meal now, and then load the ship with cheeses and drive off the best of the lambs. Our comrades will welcome us home this night, for we shall be full-handed!"

So, careless of danger, they sat them down in that perilous place and made merry on the giant's cheer. They had brought skins of wine with them, and they drank in mockery to their absent host.

In the middle of the feast one of the men suddenly laid down his cup. "Hearken," he said uneasily, "do you hear anything, friends?"

"I hear nothing," said Ulysses. "What sound did you hear?"

"A distant sound, I thought," answered the man, "as if the earth shook."

"There is nothing," said a third at length; but a certain constraint fell upon them all, and anxiety clouded their faces.

"Let us begone," said Ulysses at length. "There is what I do not like in the air. I fear evil."

He had but hardly made an end of speaking when all of them there were struck rigid with apprehension. A distant but rapidly-nearing sound assailed their ears, a heavy crunching sound like the blows of a great hammer upon the earth, save that each succeeding blow was louder than the last. They stood irresolute for one fatal moment, and then started to run towards the mouth of the cave.

The noise filled all the air, which hummed and trembled with it. They reached the entrance, but too late. Even as the first man came out into the afternoon sunlight, a great herd of cattle came pouring into the courtyard. Behind them, towering over the wall, as tall as the tallest pine on the slopes of Hymettus, strode Polyphemus, the giant king of the Cyclopes, son of the God Poseidon.

The giant was naked to the waist, where he wore a girdle of skins. One great eye burned in the centre of his forehead, and a row of sharp, white teeth were framed by thick dribbling lips, like the lips of a cow.

Under his arm Polyphemus carried a bundle of young sapling trees, which he had brought for faggots for his fire. He threw them on the floor of the courtyard by the mouth of the cave with a great crash. The adventurers crouched away at the back of the cave in the darkness as the giant entered.

He drove all the ewes of his flock before him, leaving the rams outside in the court. Then he took a great hole of rock, which scarce twenty teams of horses could have moved, and closed the mouth of the cave.

With a great sigh of weariness, which echoed like a hissing wind and blew the silent bats which hung to the roof this way and that in a frightened eddy of wings, he sank down upon his couch of skins. The giant had brought some of the firewood into the cave with him and he threw it into the embers.

A resinous piece of wood suddenly caught the flame and flared up, filling the cavern with red light. One of the sailors dropped his spear with a loud clatter as the flames made plain the figure of the monster.

Polyphemus turned his head and saw them.

He stared steadily at them with his single eye for full a minute. A cruel smile played on his face.

"Who are you, strangers?" he said at length, in a thick, low voice like the swell of a great organ. "Merchants, are you? Pirates? And whence come you along the paths of the sea?"

Then Ulysses spoke in a smooth voice of conciliation. "We are Greeks, oh lord, soldiers of

Agamemnon's army, bound for home over the seas from Troy. Bad weather has driven us out of our course, and so we have come to you and beg you to be our honoured host. Oh, great lord, have reverence for the gods, for Zeus himself is the god of hospitality."

Then the giant smiled cunningly. "You are a man of little wit, stranger," he said, "or else you have indeed come from the very end of the world. I pay no heed to Zeus, for I am stronger than he. But now, tell me, where is your ship?"

But Ulysses, the wary one, saw the snare and answered humbly, "The great Poseidon, god of the deep, wrecked our ship upon the rocks, and we alone survive of all our company."

The giant looked fixedly at the trembling band for a moment. Then, with a sudden movement, he snatched among the mariners and grasped two of them in his mighty hand.

The swift horror remained with them in all their after life. He stripped the clothes from each like a man strips the scales from a prawn with one quick twirl of his fingers.

Then he dashed the quivering bodies upon the ground so that the yellow paste of the brains smeared the stone—save for the horrid crunching of bone and flesh, and the liquid gurgle of the monster's throat as he made his frightful meal, there was no sound in the cave.

Then he fell into a foul sleep.

Three times during the long night did Ulysses

draw his sword to plunge it into the monster's heart, three times did he sheathe it again. For in his wisdom he knew that if he killed Polyphemus no one could ever move away the great stone which shut them from the outside world.

In the morning Elpenor and one other died, and the giant drove his flocks to pasture and closed up the heroes in the cave.

Then Ulysses comforted the dying hearts of his men, and as Polyphemus strode away over the hills whistling to his cattle, he made a plan for one last bid for freedom.

Leaning against the wall of the cave was a great club of hard wood which the monster had put there to dry. It was an olive-tree trunk as big as the great spar of a ship.

This they took and sharpened with their swords, and hardened it in the flame of the fire and hid it carefully away. Then very sadly the sailors cast lots as to who should be the four to help the captain. All day long they sat in the fœtid cave and prayed to the gods for an alms of aid. And their hearts were leaden for love of their valiant comrades.

At eventime two more heroes died.

Then Ulysses rose, and though his knees were weak and his face blanched with agony, he spoke in a smooth voice. "My Lord Cyclops," he said, "I have filled this bowl with wine which we brought with us. I pray you drink, and perchance your heart may be touched and you will let us go."

So the giant took the bowl from the king, and

as Ulysses went near him his breath reeked of carrion and blood. He drank the wine, which was a sweet and drowsy vintage from the Lotus Island. "Give me more," he cried thickly, "and say how you are named, for I will grant you a favour."

Ulysses filled the bowl for him three times. "Oh, my lord," he said, "my friends and parents call me Noman, for that is my name. Now, great lord, your boon."

The giant leered at the hero with drunken cunning. "Noman, since that is your name Noman, you shall die last of all, and the others first. That is your boon!"

And once more he sank into his sleep, gorged with blood and wine.

The hours wore on and the flames of the fire sank into a bright red glow. The loud stertorous breathing of the monster became more deep and regular. Very silently the five rose from among the rest and stole towards the fire with the great stake. They pressed it into the heart of the white hot embers and sat watching it change from black to crimson, while little sparks ran up and down the sides like flies upon the wall.

When the spar was just about to burst into flame they drew it out, and with quick, nervous footsteps carried it to where Polyphemus lay sleeping. The glow from the hot hard wood played upon that vast blood-smeared countenance and the yellow wrinkled lid which veiled the cruel eye.

Ulysses directed the point to the exact centre of the foul skin, and then with their old battle cry of "Helen!" the five heroes pressed it home through the hissing, steaming eyeball, turning it round and round until everything was burned away.

They had just time to leap aside when the giant rose in horrid agony. His cries of rage and pain were like the cries of a thousand tortured beasts, and the din was so great that pieces of rock began to fall from the roof of the cave. He spun round in his torture, beating upon the walls with his arms and head until they were a raw and bleeding wound.

At this awful sound mighty footsteps were heard outside the cave as the other giants rushed down from the hills. There came great and terrible voices shouting together, and it was as though a great storm was racing through the world.

"What ails you, brother, that you call us from sleep in the night?" cried the giants.

"Help! help! brothers. Noman is murdering me. I die!"

A chorus of thunderous laughter came rolling back. "If Noman harms thee, then how should we aid thee, brother? 'Tis the gods who have sent thee a sickness which thou must endure."

And now, through an aperture high up in the cave, the light began to whiten, and showed day was at hand. The footsteps of the Cyclopes grew faint and ceased, but Polyphemus lay moaning by the great stone which closed the entrance.

The morning light grew stronger, and a breeze stole in, fresh and clean, and played upon the faces of the prisoners.

The ewes began to bleat, for their milking time was at hand, and the rams cried out for freedom and the green pastures of the hill.

The giant moved aside the stone to let them go and in the morning sunlight the sailors could see that he felt over them with his hands so that no men should mingle with them and so escape.

First the ewes went out and then the young rams, and last of all the great old rams, patriarchs of the flock, began to move slowly towards the door.

Then courage came back to Ulysses, and with it all his cunning. Stooping low under the belly of a great beast, he motioned to his friends to do likewise, and, slowly, in this way, holding to the fleece of the rams, they moved out of the cave. They could feel the rams tremble when the giant's hands ranged over the wool of their backs, but nevertheless they came safely out into the light, and stole down to where their ship yet lay at anchor.

The air of the morning was like wine to them, and the face of the water as dear as the face of a well-beloved wife as they ran over the bright yellow sand.

Then from the stern of the boat Ulysses cried out in a great voice of triumph. At that sound the monster came stumbling from his cave, reeling like a drunken man, and calling on his father

Poseidon, Lord of the Sea, to avenge him on his enemies. He took up the stone that had barred the cave and threw it far out into the water, but it overshot the boat and did not harm the heroes, though the wave of its descent flung the ship from side to side as if it were a piece of driftwood. The mariners bent to the oars, and the vessels moved away from that accursed shore, slowly at first but more swiftly as their tired arms grew strong with the chance of safety, and the wine of hope flowed in their veins once more.

They saw the sightless face of Polyphemus working horribly, his mouth opening and shutting like a dying fish as he looked heavenwards and implored his mighty father's aid.

And after a space of mourning for the brave dead the heroes set out again over the sad grey seas, seeking Ithaca.

But the heart of King Ulysses was sick and weary, for he dreaded the wrath to come, and most of all he longed for home.

THE SECOND EPISODE

The Adventure of the Palace in the Wood

Ulysses slowly mounted the wooded hill. The path which rose towards the summit wound in and out through thick undergrowth, and his feet made no sound upon the green moss of the track.

He had his spear ready for any game that he might chance on, but for half a day he saw no living thing save a few mailed lizards that lay open-eyed upon a stone.

No birds twittered in the forest on the mountainside, only the wild bees sang in the stillness like jewels with voices.

How beautiful the wood was! and how mysterious also. Ulysses felt a quickening of the pulses which did not come from fear, and a strange excitement possessed him which arose from he knew not what cause.

The trees in the forest were very old and grew thickly together. The trunks were painted delicate greens, greys and browns by lichens, and the foliage overhead met and made a roof of bright leaves. Beneath this canopy there was a sort of twilight like the gloom in the temple of Zeus at Sparta.

Ulysses toiled on and up. After a time the trees began to open out and grow less thickly. The moss-carpet began to be rocky and uneasy to walk upon, so that Ulysses knew that he must be nearing the top.

At last he climbed a few worn boulders and stood alone upon the peak. From that great height he could discern the sea on all sides of the island. Beyond the thick woodlands below, the yellow sands of the shore went out to meet the water, and the king could see the ship riding at anchor and a small boat plying from it to a tiny group of black dots upon the beach.

Ulysses sent his gaze circling slowly over the unbroken green of the woods. When his roving glance fell upon the very centre of the island he started suddenly and shaded his eyes from the sunlight with both hands. A thick column of blue smoke was rising from among the trees, and looking more intently than before he could see the gleam of white marble here and there through the greenwood, and catch the sunlight glinting upon copper.

He had learned what he came to know; there was life upon the island. But of what kind? Did some fearful monster lurk yonder, three miles away in the forest. Another Cyclops, perchance, or some angry god wroth at a disturbance of his privacy.

The still smoke rose into the soft air and a great calm seemed to brood over the place. No birds flew about the roofs.

He began to retrace his steps down towards his comrades on the shore to tell them what he had seen.

The wood was as still as before, but when he came to the meadow lands below he dropped quickly behind a clump of fern, for his keen eyes had seen a smooth brown flank not far away. A great stag was drinking at a little stream which sang its way down from the mountain to the sea. They had touched at the island with very little food left, and the king had promised that he would return with spoils from hunting.

Just as the beast raised his head from the water the spear flashed like a gleam of light from the clump of fern, and the quarry stumbled, clattering among the stones with a sob.

Then Ulysses made a rope of willow twigs and tied the stag's feet together and brought him to the ship.

Only half the crew were upon the shore, for the rest had gone to explore the inward parts of the island with Eurylochus as their leader.

They skinned the stag and made a fire, and roasted the sweet flesh upon their spear points. While they sat eating, a man with a white face came running over the shore towards them, and as they saw him come they rose with their arms in fear, for they knew that once more they had come to some dangerous and evil place, and that a deadly peril lurked in the forest.

They saw he who ran was Eurylochus, and that he ran in terror.

But none followed him in pursuit, nor did any arrow come singing like a bee from the shelter of the neighbouring trees.

Eurylochus rushed up to them and sank exhausted by the fire. Ulysses gave him wine, and motioned the others to ask no questions but to let the man tell his tale in his own way. For he knew it would be more vivid so.

"More evil, comrades!" he sobbed out at last, "and good men and true lost to us for ever. Know you where we have landed? This accursed place is Ææa, the home of the Goddess Circe, and I have seen her face to face."

Ulysses started violently, and despair crept into his eyes as he motioned Eurylochus to proceed.

"We went up through the valleys," said the lieutenant, "and entered the wood. After we had walked long, and were thirsty and weary, we came to an open glade in which stood the house of Circe. It was built of polished marble with copper roofs, and the trees made a thick wall on all sides of the glade. A very strange, silent place! All round the house were lions and mountain wolves playing with each other. We turned to fly in fear, but the beasts fawned upon us with gentle paws and waving tails, and we saw their eyes were sad and tame, and they were all unlike the beasts of the field. They were as dogs at supper begging for food from their masters. But it was an awful sight nevertheless.

"Now, as we stood waiting in the porch, we heard a sweet low song inside the palace, sweeter

than any mortal song, like the flutes and harps of the gods. Then we looked in, and we saw the goddess weaving at a golden loom, and going up and down before it as she sang. And Polites—oh, dear Polites!—called out to her, and the song ceased, and Circe came out to us, and bade us enter, and her beauty was like moonlight. Then the men went in, but I remained, mindful of the Cyclops and fearing harm. So I sat down in the wood, and the beasts played round me, and the lions licked my hands with their hard rough tongues. But I could see what was toward in the palace hall.

"The goddess led them to rich couches and chairs, and she prepared a drink for them of golden honey and purple wine, white fresh cheese, and meal of corn. But she poured a brew of magic herbs into the drink, and when they had passed the bowl from hand to hand and drunk she waved a wand of cedar wood over them."

He stopped, choking with emotion and shaking with horror at what he had seen. He covered his face with his hands.

Ulysses placed a firm hand upon his shoulder, and he took up his tale once more. "And when she waved her wand behold a horror! For suddenly my comrades dwindled, and were changed to swine. The bristles of swine grew out upon them, and they grunted like swine, but still the souls of men shone out of their eyes. And she drove them away into a pen, and threw them beech nuts, laughing most musically. And I,

the unhappy one, fled and am come hither with my tale."

Ulysses rose with a pale set face, and stern hard lines flashed out round his lips. For a moment he prayed in silence to Athene. Then he slung his strung bow upon his shoulder, and loosened the arrows in the quiver, testing each one for a flaw in the shaft. He took his great silver-studded sword and buckled it round his waist. "I alone, my comrades, must go to the palace of the enchantress," he said. "I have no choice but to go and strive. May the gods preserve you, friends."

He was preparing to move away when they all entreated him to remain with them, but he would not listen, and as he moved away and was lost to their sight they broke out into loud praises of him among themselves.

It was ever thus. Their father and captain was first in wisdom and courage, and had always seemed to them more god than man.

Ulysses passed over the meadows with slow sure step, thinking deeply. The forest closed about him, dark and lonely, and his walk changed. He became alert, walking warily and softly. His keen eyes roved over the untrodden paths, seeking to pierce the mystery of the greenwood.

He had halted by a brook for a moment, debating which path he should venture, when help came to him.

There was a crash in the tree tops above him, a glittering ball of light fell through the green,

and a wind rushed among the leaves, suddenly rousing all the voices of the wood.

A young and beautiful man, holding a golden rod, with a slight down upon his lip, came towards him.

Ulysses knew that the God Hermes had flashed down from heaven to be his counsellor. He fell upon his knees before the divine messenger.

"The great Athene has sent me to you, king," said the god, "for she heard your prayer upon the shore, and will deliver you from the forest danger. Here is a sprig of the magic herb moly. Take it in your hand for a safeguard against the wiles of Circe.

"When you go into the palace she will mix you her enchanted potion, and strike you with her wand. Do you draw your sword, and make as though to slay her. Then she will fear greatly and swear to do you no harm."

Ulysses took the white flowered talisman, and Hermes vanished among the trees.

Then he came swiftly upon the gleaming palace, and going up to the marble porch struck upon it with his sword hilt, and called to the goddess.

She glimmered towards him. Her hair was like a young horse-chestnut fresh from the pod. Her eyes were like pools of violet water, her neck was a tower of ivory, and her lips were red as sunset.

The flower of evil, the goddess of strange sins!

She smiled at the hero, and led him by the hand to a table on which was a golden cup, proffering it to him in welcome.

Ulysses bowed low before her loveliness, and as he drank there was a strange smile in his eyes.

The enchantress looked at him steadily. For a single moment a ripple of doubt crossed her face, but suddenly she seized her cedarn rod and smote his side, crying, "Get you to the stye, and lie there in filth with your companions."

Ulysses drew his great sword, and held it over her with menacing eyes. She drooped to him, a very woman! and clung round him, weeping, and he could feel her warm heart beating, beating close to his. Her lovely hair fell around her in a golden cloud, and tears streamed down her cheeks as she swore by the gods on the Holy Hill never to harm him.

And looking on her sinful loveliness the brain of Ulysses burned for her, and he took her lithe body in his strong arms and pressed the blossom of her lips to his. Her arms stole round him, and she called him lord and king.

Then with a soft smile she led him to the courtyard where the swine lay sleeping in the sun. When the foul beasts saw Ulysses they set up a horrid chorus of grunting, and he raged to see his valiant friends so degraded. But clinging to him, the goddess raised her hand, and the swine vanished, and the goodly mariners stood up among the straw, more straight and tall than before, with all the marks of hardship and travel smoothed from their faces.

That night the other mariners came up from the shore, guided by Ulysses. And the amber lamps

flared in the hall, and all night till daybreak they made a great feast. They sang in praise of love and wine, and Circe sat at the right hand of the King of Ithaca.

When the rosy dawn rushed up the sky, the goddess rose.

The lamps paled in the fresh new light, and the feast was over.

The mariners lay in sleep about the board, and the purple wine was spilt about them.

Only the Goddess and the Hero were awake.

Then she said, "Lord and love, the night is over. The sun climbs the sky, the woodlands awake. But let us go into my scented chamber, my purple chamber where the day never comes. There will we lie in love and sleep and forget the day."

She led him by the hand over the cool marble floor. The purple curtains fell behind them with a soft noise of falling. All sound was hushed in the courts of the palace, and the whole house was still.

THE THIRD EPISODE

How Ulysses walked in Hell, and of the Adventure of the Sirens and Scylla

The King of Ithaca stood all alone on a gloomy barren shore, spear in hand. The sky lowered black overhead, and from the vast yawning hole in the terrible cliff which rose up before him he seemed to hear strange wailings and faint cries coming, so it seemed, from a great distance.

Had he at last broken away from the loving arms of Circe for this horror? Stung once more by the latent manhood in his blood, he had roused his energies and left the enchanted island to set out once more upon the weary quest for home. He had bade the goddess farewell and sailed away from the island of sweet lust to seek a ghostly counsellor and to drink deep at that fountain of wisdom which was once the glory of Thebes.

When Circe had bade him, if he would indeed get back to Ithaca and leave her arms, seek the dead Tiresias in the place of the dead it had seemed an easy thing.

What were pale ghosts to a warrior of Troyland and the vanquisher of Polyphemus? If the old seer

alone could tell him how to conquer the wrath of Poseidon and win to his wife's arms once more, should he not go with a will?

And he had set out with his crew, and the magic wind which Circe gave them had brought them hither over grey sad seas, while they had touched nor oars nor helm.

And now Ulysses went slowly up to the fissure in the rock, but a long solitary cry made him reel back trembling as his brave heart had never done before.

Then he was, in an instant moment, aware of a more than mortal presence. Into that dread place came the awful majesty of the Queen of Heaven, and he fell to the ground before Athene.

The full flowing river of her speech came down upon him.

"If thou wouldst hold thy wife once more, Ulysses, and see thy rocky western home, then must thou dare this peril. None can help thee now save thou thyself. So it is decreed by the gods. If so be it that thy courage fails thee now then wilt thou be a wanderer for ever."

"Lady of Heaven," he said, "I dare not go. Oh, anything but that."

"Penelope!" she murmured sweetly.

"I cannot face the dead."

"Ithaca."

"Oh, listen to those wailings in the abyss!"

"Thy father Laertes weeps yet for the wanderer."

"The dead! The dead are waiting there!"

"Men call thee Ulysses!" said the goddess, and at that word something moved within him and his limbs began to stiffen, and once more the hero felt the spear-shank hard and cold within his grasp.

He raised his face, and there was once more the old proud light upon it. Athene had gone, and big with his new resolve he stepped towards the blackness.

A voice came to him, thin, and far down.

"Ulysses! Ulysses! son of Laertes, I wait to guide thee. Hermes, son of Zeus, is with thee. Take courage in both hands and come."

The king moved forward, and the dark swallowed him up. He stumbled along a descending rock-strewn pathway. In the increasing gloom it seemed to him that he was on the side of a steep hill. A moaning wind encircled him. Now and again a slight gleam was visible from the golden helmet of the god.

Far far down he saw the leaden livid river of death, and on the sullen tide floated the stately funeral barge of Charon, the ferryman of the dead.

The wind grew even more mournful and sad as they trod the meadows of asphodel and the grey lilies of the underworld towards the marge of Styx.

Then the god called out aloud to the ferryman. As his voice echoed over the water, the dusky night became full of the sound of wings, and dark shapes filled the air. The spirits of the dead flapped round them in continual movement.

The ghosts began to call and cry to the living hero. Some had little squeaky voices like bats, others made a louder and more hollow sound.

The howlings of the formless increased all round Ulysses.

The inarticulate found utterance in the indefinite.

The waves of weird and hopeless voices rose, fell, undulated, now loud and shrill, now sobbing into silence. Little eager whispers filled the hero's ear.

And to the terror of these great murmurs were added the sight of superhuman outlines, which melted away in the gloom almost as they appeared. Alecto and Tisiphone, the Furies, circled round Ulysses, and Megeara flew through the dark to her sisters.

A cold hand seemed placed upon the hero's soul. Cries from precipice to precipice, from air to water, went on unceasingly—the melancholy vociferations of the lost!

The loquacity of Hell!

And in deadly fear, but resolute still, Ulysses struggled on through this great twilight world, open on all sides. As he walked on, the flying outlaws of the tomb seemed to be swarming over him and pressing him to the ground. He struggled beneath the weight of lost souls, but his whirling arms struck nothing but the empty air.

Fresh clouds of spirits pricked the twilight, increased in size, amalgamated, thickened, and hurried towards him, crying.

They came to the brink of the river. Before them, as they looked out over the water, was no horizon, but an opaque lividity like a wan, moving precipice, a cliff of the night.

Then the old man Charon bowed to the commands of the gods and embarked them on his barge. He gazed on Ulysses with his keen wicked eyes, and his long white beard wagged in hideous mockery at this mortal among the dead.

The thin pole dipped in and out of the water, and the drops which fell from it were the colour of leaden bullets, for there is no life in the water of Styx.

Ulysses knelt in the bottom of the boat and shut out Hell from his eyes with his hand. He prayed to Athene for help to endure, and that he might have an answer from the old Seer Tiresias that would lead him safely home at last.

And now the other bank of the river began to loom up before them and the air began to be silent.

On the bank, as it seemed to welcome them, stood a tall old man with a golden sceptre in his hand. His face was full of an unutterable sadness, and his eyes were horny and dim with blindness. But his magic staff conducted him safely to the river brink, and in a high shivering voice he hailed Ulysses.

"Why hast thou come here, O wise one, leaving the happy daylight for this cheerless shore? Noble son of Laertes, I know thy quest, and thus make answer. Father Zeus gave me power, which

still remains, and I, an old blind ghost, can see into the future even on the shores of Styx. Thou seekest to know if thou wilt ever catch thy wife in thy strong arms once more, and tread the well-beloved fields of Ithaca. The mighty god of the sea, Poseidon, is wroth with thee and a malevolent god. For even now his son Polyphemus stumbles a bruised and sightless way among his native hills. But yet you may return after long woes and heavy toil. But one thing bear well in mind, O king, else wilt thou suffer unbelievable things. When thy ship touches at the Island Thrinacia, great herds of cattle will be feeding there on the fresh sweet grass which grows in the goodly upper world. These be the beeves and steers of the divine Helios, the Sun-God, and must be inviolate to men. But if one sacred beast is slain, then thy ship and all thy company will perish.

"Perchance thou thyself may win Ithaca forlorn, and to find others in thy place, but that I know not. I have spoken."

Then with a long melancholy cry the figure vanished into the dark.

But in its place came a shadowy form which made the heart of the hero leap and beat, so it seemed all Hades was filled with the tumult.

His mother Anticlea stood before him.

Stretching out her cold, thin hands she spoke.

"My boy that I suckled, why hast thou come into Hades not yet being dead, for I see that the flesh is still warm upon thee for which I drank to Zeus?"

"Mother of mine, I sought Tiresias the Theban prophet. I have not even yet won Ithaca nor seen the dear ones there. A god is against me. So I came through the spirits of the unburied, and over the dark river to seek counsel of the seer. Knowest thou in this beyond-earth if the beloved Penelope still holds me in her heart? or is she perhaps here with thee, lost to the sunlight?"

The mother of Ulysses answered, "Penelope is as faithful and true as on thy wedding day, but she is in a peril, so haste ye home. And now farewell." Where Ulysses had seen his mother, was but a little grey vapour which swayed and vanished.

Then the hero called roughly to Charon, and bade him take the pole and urge the barge back to the starting-place. This time, though the multitude of the dead circled over him with cries, begging his help to take them out of Hades, he felt no fear, for his mind was burning with other thoughts.

He mounted the long cliff side, and at last in the distance saw a faint gleam of light stealing down towards him. In the pale gleam the figure of Hermes was manifest for a moment flitting up to the day before him.

The cries grew fainter and more faint. The light changed from grey to primrose, from primrose to yellow. The little star which was the mouth of the cave became a sun and then a world, and the yellow turned into the white hot sunshine as Hell faded utterly away.

On the beach the little blue waves sang on the yellow sand. The black divers rose lazily on the swell, and the shields round the prow of the ship shone like white fire.

Once more the vessel of heroes swam over the seas. And now there was another quality in the wind for them, and the world was a new world.

Their leader had told them that if they obeyed his commands they would win home once more. The news he had brought back from Hades made them sturdy and strong of heart, and they vowed that in all things they would trust in the king who had dared the perils of the underworld.

Their thoughts turned with a lover's thirst to images of their native land, tranquil skies, the old-remembered meadows, cool brooks, and eternal peace after their long wandering.

Hope beat high in the heart of Ulysses also. The grey nightmare of Hell was over and in the past, one more memory when in his own halls he would weave his saga.

He had been near to the awful thing Death.

He had found that after all it was only Death.

The ship with a fair wind ran up a lane of light into the setting sun, and when at length the moon had risen and silvered all the sea, Ulysses called the men round him.

"Comrades," he said, "with the dawn, if I have kept the reckoning aright, we shall come to the island where the Sirens dwell. Now the Lady Circe warned me against the Sirens, the singers who charm all men with their song. He who listens to Parthenope, Ligeia and Leucosia must stay with them for ever, listening spellbound to the song until he dies. And the island is covered with the bones of dead men. To listen is to die. But I wish to hear the voices and to escape the enchantment, and so obey my commands. When we near the island do you all close your ears with wax so that no sound can reach your brains. And take a stout rope and bind me to the mast so that I can in no wise loose myself. And howsoever I may order or entreat you to let me go to the Sirens, if their magic song enchants me, take no heed, but row steadily onwards until the island is far astern. Then only may you set me free."

As dawn came, a faint grey line upon the horizon showed itself on the starboard bow. At the sight, with some laughter, for it was difficult to believe in the perils of sweet music!—even for men who had seen the wonders that they had seen—the men began to press yellow wax from the honeycomb into each other's ears.

Then when no one among them could hear the flapping of the sail or the voice of the sea, nor could tell the meaning of his neighbour's voice, they went up to Ulysses, and with many light-hearted jests bound him to the mast, and because his strength was well known to them they reeved the rope with a treble hitch. No living man could have escaped from such bonds.

As sailors will, they treated the whole thing as a huge jest, making a mock mutiny of it as they
bound the captain. Ulysses could not help smiling at their mirth.

After such wise precaution he had no fear, and in his heart of hearts he did not believe that the song of the Sirens would affect him much, though he followed the advice of Circe and made himself a prisoner.

But a fierce curiosity possessed him. He cursed the slowness of the wind, for, as they bound him, the island was still a low line without colour on the water, and called out to the men to row faster, forgetting that they could not hear him.

Slowly the grey island became purple, then brown, and at last showed itself a green, low, pleasant land, a place of meadows.

The wind was behind them, and until they came quite close under the lee of the island Ulysses could hear no voices but those of the wind and waves. Then faintly at first, but rapidly becoming more sonorous and sweet, he heard the magic voices which were to ring in his ears in all his after life.

No words of his at any time could express the loveliness of those voices, of the unutterable sweetness of it, nothing.

The strains floated over the still sea like harps of heaven.

All that man had known or desired in life, all the emotions which had stirred the human heart, were blended in those magic voices. The world had nothing more to give; here, here at last, was the absolute fulfilment of beauty.

Louder and more piercingly sweet, as the unconscious sailors bent to the oars in earnest, and the sweat ran down their bare brown backs.

"Whither away, whither away, whither away? Fly no more. Whither away from the high green field, and the happy blossoming shore? Day and night to the billow the fountain calls: Down shower the gambolling waterfalls From wandering over the lea."

The face of Ulysses grew wan and grey as the ship passed a projecting point of rock. On the smooth green turf the three singers were standing. In face and form they were sweet and lovely girls.

Naked to the waist, they wore long flowing draperies below, and as they sung the rosy bosoms rose and fell with the music, and the lucid throats rippled with song.

"Mariner, mariner, furl your sails, For here are blissful downs and dales, And merrily, merrily carol the gales, And the spangle dances in bight and bay, And the rainbow forms and flies on the land Over the islands free; And the rainbow lives in the curve of the sand; Hither, come hither and see."

And still the ship went on, but more slowly, as it were some force were at work deadening the arms of the rowers.

Then the shrill loveliness fired the hero's blood, and he knew that he must go to the three lovely singers on the strand. Earth held nothing better than this—to lie for ever with that music in his ears.

"Whither away? listen and stay: mariner, mariner, fly no more."[1]

[1] These few lines of the Sirens' song have been taken from Lord Tennyson's beautiful poem "The Sea Fairies."

Then, as if drawn by the long cadenced notes as by cords, Ulysses gathered up his mighty strength and strove with his bonds.

But the sailors had done their work too well, and the rope only cut deeply into the flesh.

The white arms were stretched out to him in supplication, the song grew more full of unearthly beauty than before—and the ship was slowly passing by.

Ulysses called out to the crew in an agony of command and entreaty.

One of the men happened to look up and saw his face. He grinned, nudged his companion, and turned away.

The song grew fainter, the three tall figures dwindled. The face of Ulysses grew ashen, and when at length they came to him and cut the ropes he said no word.

He went alone to the prow of the vessel and looked out over the fair sun-bathed sea, and there were tears in his eyes, and his mouth was softer and more tremulous than it was wont to be.

So they came away from Parthenope, Ligeia and Leucosia, the Sirens.

The next day Ulysses called the crew together as before and told them of the new peril that
awaited them. For the wise Circe had warned him that after the island of the Sirens he must needs encounter the terrible Scylla, for the ship must pass by her lair on its passage towards Home.

But Ulysses knew that it was impossible to fight the monster, and that some of the crew were fated to die, but in his wisdom he did not tell them that.

He finished his speech as follows:—"And so, my friends, the gods ordain that we must face Scylla, and the whirlpool Charybdis. There is no other way. But courage! always have courage. I who brought you safe from out of the cave of the Cyclops will bring you safe from this also. And so onward and have stout hearts."

It was a misty day, and everything was shadowy and faint, but the ship moved slowly along a sheer wall of black cliff which towered up above them for a thousand feet or more. The top was lost in the mist. It was a lowering, frightful place.

One of the sailors gave a shout which echoed back to them in mournful mockery through the mist.

They rowed on steadily, hugging the cliff. Ulysses stood in the prow of the boat. He had put on armour and took two spears in his hand.

His eyes searched the face of the cliff till they ached from the minute scrutiny.

This waiting for the inevitable was terribly unnerving. Ulysses himself, knowing that some must die, was heavy and sad at heart as they glided along the side of the cliff.

To the left the great whirlpool seethed and boiled, its outermost convolution scarce a bow-shot away. When it threw up the water the spray dashed up a hundred feet and fell in showers over the sailors, and as the water ran back in the ebb Ulysses could see, far down the black and spinning sides, to where the old witch Charybdis dwelt on the dark sand of the sea bottom.

Suddenly the end came. A loud barking and howling startled them all so that each man paused on his oar. A pack of hounds were unkenneled, so it seemed, somewhere on the cliff face in the mist.

Then a sickly musky smell enveloped them, so foul and stale that they coughed and spat even as their blood ran cold with fear.

Through the curtain of mist, which had suddenly grown very thick, six objects loomed right over the boat.

Six long tentacles swayed and quivered over the sailors, and at the end of each was a grinning head set with cruel fangs and a little red eager tongue that flickered in and out.

For a moment the heads hung poised, and then each sought and found its victim.

Six sailors were slowly drawn out of the boat, shrieking the name of Ulysses for the last time in their death agony. And all the time the barking of the hounds in the obscene womb of the monster went on unceasingly.

Then the fury of flight came upon them. With bursting brains and red fire before their eyes they

laboured at the great oars until the wood bent and shook and the ship leaped forward like a driven horse.

And they left the strait of death and came out of the mist into a wide sunlit sea. But still a sound of distant barking came down the wind.

So Scylla took her horrid toll of heroes.

But Ulysses called them to prayer and lamentation for the dead.

THE FOURTH EPISODE

How Ulysses lost his Merry Men and came A Waif to Calypso with the Shining Hair

The crew sat round a fire of driftwood.

There was shelter where they sat, in a natural alcove of rock, but outside the great winds thundered and the wrack flew before the storm and a mighty unceasing roar filled the air.

The faces of all the sailors wore a sullen look. Hunger had begun to suck the colour from their cheeks, their eyes were prominent and strained, their movements without energy or vigour.

A rude shelter of sailcloth and various *débris* that was scattered about seemed to show that for some time, at least, they had made their home in this place where the winds did not come.

Ulysses was not among them. They were talking in low, discontented tones among themselves.

"A whole month," said Eurylochus, "a whole month have we been sea bound in this accursed island. I am sick of islands!"

"Never have we put to shore without some evil thing befalling," said another. "Oh, for Ithaca!"

"I doubt we shall ever see Ithaca again," said a third. "We will be wanderers till we die; that is what I think. And this place is like to be the grave of all of us. I never knew a wind so furious to blow so long. We should sink in an hour did we but put out."

"There is only food for one day more, and that sparse," said Eurylochus. "For my part, my limbs are heavy as brass and the strength is all gone from me. I could not move an oar now. Man needs meat and wine or the fires of hunger burn the sinews and dry the blood. Brown meat and red wine! I could fill my belly till the skin cracked!"

"The rich brown meat, mate! Dost mind the soft kids on Circe's island? By Zeus, I can taste them now!"

"Ay and the fat cows, roast till the blood ran out of them like liquid life."

"I can even smell the smell of the roasting meat now. A welcome smell to a hungry man."

"Would that we had never left Circe. 'Twas a kind queen, meet for our master! but her girls were kindly in love also."

"To Hades with the girls!" said Eurylochus. "Thy talk of meat makes me heave with desire."

He looked round cautiously before he continued.

"Friends," he said in a low, rapid whisper, "tell me, are ye purposing to starve in the midst of

plenty? Saw ye ever such fat oxen and cows as graze in the pastures above?"

"Never did I see such cattle," answered another hungry wight. "Gods! they would make a feast for kings."

"And yet pain and sickness is all over us, and we lust for food till we know not what we do!"

"Captain's orders!"

"Ulysses has lost his cunning for sure, and hunger has turned his brain. He is no more the brave leader of old. He goes wandering alone among the rocks and sleeps all day. And his eye is clouded and courage has left his voice. Friends, shall we die thus? No man of ye loveth Ulysses better than I love him. Is he not my kinsman indeed? He brought us from the Cyclops' cave and dared the perils of Hell. All this I know and say before you now. But the king is distraught and moody. He does not know what he is doing. He would be the first to join us with the merry and grateful word were he to come back and find the good red beef roasting on the fire and smell the savoury smoke."

"Ay, captain was never one set against a feast! He loves good cheer, as becomes a proper fighting man."

"My mind doubts me, comrades," said another. "Should we not rather trust the king even unto this last thing? Have we ever found him wanting yet? Did he not make us promise? Zeus knows if the thought of hot meat does not tickle my belly as well as thine—more, friend, for thou hast

a paunch yet and none have I—but I for one trust in the captain. He knows."

Then Eurylochus took up his spear as if he had decided and the discussion was over.

"Listen, men," he said. "In all shapes death is a terrible thing. But I would rather die quickly at Scylla's hands than fade into Hades through famine. Hunger is the worst death of all. Come with me and bring your spears. We will choose the best of the herd and sacrifice to the gods.

When we reach home again, can we not build a great temple to Helios, and fill it with rich gifts? The Sun-God, who gives light to all the world, will not grudge us a cow or two. Not he. 'Tis a more genial god than that. Ay, and though we indeed anger the god and he wreck us in the deep! I put ye this question—Would ye not rather swallow the cold salt water for a moment and so die, than die for days among the rocks?"

His pale face worked with the force of his words. His eyes glistened with a terrible eagerness. As he spoke in a high, quivering nervous tenor, shaking his spear at them, the eagerness crept into their eyes also.

Famine strangely transforms the human face. They became men with brute's eyes.

Eurylochus marched away out of the shelter towards the pasture lands, and the others followed him. New strength seemed to come to them as they walked towards the herd, which could be seen, a red brown mass, grazing on a plain some half-mile away.

The full force of the wind struck and retarded them as they emerged into the open, but it brought the lowing of the cattle to their ears and they pressed on.

Ulysses lay sleeping about a quarter of a mile from the cove.

He had wandered away from his companions in great despondency. For four long weeks the gale had roared past the island away to the north. The rain had fallen like spears, the thunder stammered its awful message, the green and white lightning snapped like whips of light. In all this the king saw the finger of evil. He knew that the mighty Poseidon still watched his fortunes with cruel, angry eyes. For this storm was no chance warring of the elements, but came, he knew, directed against him and his fated crew.

Food had got lower and lower, the men began to grumble, and black looks of reproach met his eyes on every side.

And all the time the fat cattle of Apollo cropped the tender shoots of the grass, the full udder dropped with creamy milk, and the shining flanks of the great beasts sent an alluring message to the starving men.

Often Ulysses withdrew into some lonely place and prayed to Athene, but she seemed asleep or weary of his woes, for there came no answering sign.

On this day hope seemed to have utterly departed from him. There was no break in the leaden clouds of the future.

He had wandered away along the seashore, and fallen asleep from languor and grief, lulled by the great singing of the gale overhead.

In his sleep he dreamed vividly. He saw the interior of the island. Suddenly, from among a clump of trees, a bright beam of golden light shot up heavenwards. He knew that one of the shepherd nymphs of Apollo went with some message for the god, and he shivered and moaned in his slumber.

Then it seemed that he was in a great place of cloud, an immense formless world of mist. And through the mist came a terrible voice which turned him to stone. It was the voice of Apollo crying in anger.

"Oh, Father Zeus, and all ye gods who dwell upon the hill above the thunder! punish the comrades of Ulysses for their crime. They have speared my beautiful cows that were my joy and of which I had great pleasure. Whenever I turned my face and shone upon the world I watched them feeding in my island. And now these whelps have slain the finest of all my herd. Vengeance! Bitter vengeance, or will I go far down into Hell and leave the world in gloom and shine no more upon it. I will make Hades a place of warmth and laughter, and the world all grey and full of death."

In the midst Ulysses awoke with that angry cry still ringing in his ears. With a sick apprehension he hurried along the slippery boulders to the shelter place where he had left the crew.

Within a hundred yards of the place he knew the worst. The wind blew a savoury smoke towards him, and his stomach yearned while his brain trembled in fear.

The men were in high glee when he came round the corner of rock among them, great joints turned upon rough spits, skins and horns encumbered the ground, and the rich fat dropped hissing into the fire.

A sudden silence fell upon their merriment as the captain came. He spread out his hands with a gesture of despair.

"Comrades," he said sorrowfully, "ye have chosen to do this thing against my advice, and now it is done we must abide by the deed. I cannot reproach you. Still, I know that we must pay heavily for this sin against the Sun-God. Farewell, Ithaca! And now it is over let us eat of our unhallowed spoil. It may be that this is our last meal together, comrades."

As he had finished speaking a strange and ominous thing happened. The blood-stained skins began to creep about like live things upon the ground.

The red meat over the fire withered and moaned as if in pain. The air was filled with a lowing as of cows.

Then in mad fear and riotous despair they fell upon the horrid meal with eager, tremulous hands. Ulysses was taken with the madness like the rest, and until sundown they gorged the dripping meat till they could eat no more, and

their faces were bloated and their eyes were strained.

As the sun sank into the sea with a red and angry face the wind dropped and ceased. A great calm spread over the waters. When the moon rose the ocean was like a sheet of still silver.

Very hurriedly, whispering among themselves, as though they were afraid of their own voices, they launched the ship and rowed out into the moonlight, racing away from the accursed isle.

And now the last scene of all came very quickly.

Ulysses was wont to say that of all the things he had witnessed in his life this was the saddest and most terrible.

A sudden crackle of thunder pealed over the sky. A fantastic network of lightning played round the ship like lace.

A dark cloud formed itself directly over the boat, not two mast's lengths above, and all the waves below became like ink in the shadow. For a time it hung there motionless, and then suddenly a mighty wind swooped down on them like a hawk drops out of the sky. The mast snapped like a pipe-stem and crashed upon the deck, braining the helmsman in its fall. A smooth green wave, just slightly bubbling with froth on the crest, but like a hill of oil, rose and swept over the ship.

Ulysses clung to a stanchion with all his mighty strength, and was just able to battle against the flood. When it passed over him he saw that every man of the crew was in the water. For

a few moments they floated round him with sad cries of farewell, and then one by one they were swept into the Ultimate.

The timbers of the ship broke away and she fell to pieces. With a loud cry to Athene, Ulysses launched himself on the waves clinging to a great log which had formed part of the keel. A swift current urged him along far away from the scene of the wreck.

The purpose of the god was accomplished, and the waves fell, and the moonlight shone out clear and still once more.

On all the waste of waters no sail, no cape nor headland broke the silver monotone.

Loneliness descended upon the hero like a cloak; an utter abandonment such as he had never known before in life.

The water began to grow very cold.

An awful silence lay over the sea. The terrible jubilant silence of a god revenged!

"And so all those well-known, long-tried voices were still! Never again would Eurylochus drain the full tankard in a kindly health."

Ulysses bowed his head, and bitter tears welled up into his eyes.

"Never again would grey old Diphilos stand at the helm of the good ship, sending his keen eyes out over the sounding wastes. How the last mournful cry of Jamenos had echoed through the storm. Young, straight Jamenos who had approached the Cyclops with him, beautiful young Jamenos, with the bold eyes and curling hair!

And there was old Perdix too, old Perdix with his grin and chuckle and his tales. Never would Perdix sit by the fire and make merry yarns any more. The little twinkling rat-like eyes were stark and glazed now. Perdix stood beside the livid river among the rushing spirits. He would have no jests now."

He saw them all together, in peril, storm, and quiet weather. His trusty men! His dear comrades!

And now he alone was left, alone, alone, alone.

Perhaps Athene herself was still with him and had not even yet forgotten her wanderer. As the thought struck along his brain a faint blush of hope began to flush his pallid cheek.

He floated on and on. Dawn came, waxed strong, waned. Tremulous evening came like a shy novice about to take the veil of night. Night blazed in moonlit splendour once more.

And at the hour when night stands still and dawn is not yet, the waves, kindlier than before, carried him to the island of Ogygia, where he heard the sea nymphs on the shore singing him a fairy welcome.

Soft hands drew him from the deep, soft voices welcomed him; it seemed as if one queenly presence, a tall woman with golden hair which shone, towered among the rest, and he fell into a gentle swoon, a soft surrender to sleep.

"We watch the fleeting isles of shade That float upon the sea When 'neath the sun some cloud hath spread His purple canopy. The woodbine odours scent the air, The cypress' leaves are wet From meadow springs that rise among Parsley and violet. Here shall the Wanderer remain; The land of Love's Delight; Shall here forget the past, the old Sad spectres of the night."

Soft and low the sea-maidens sang while Ulysses lay sleeping—even as they had sung nine long years ago when the sea cast him up on the shores of Calypso's kingdom.

It was bright sunlight, a great fire of cedar wood burnt on an altar before the cave of the goddess who loved the hero, and the smoke scented all the island.

Among the grove of stately trees which bordered the smooth pneumatic lawn in front of the cave Ulysses lay sleeping on a bed of fresh-born violets. A purple mantle shot with gold, woven by Calypso, was spread over him.

The poplars and fragrant cypresses were full of sweet-voiced birds.

Over the mouth of the cave grew a great vine, and the black grapes drooped and fell from it in their abundance.

From the centre of the short emerald grass four springs of clear water came up in thin whips and flowed away in flashing rivulets.

This was the home and kingdom of the Goddess

Calypso, and was so beautiful a place that the fame of it had even reached Olympus, and the gods knew of the island.

And nine long years had passed! It was nine years ago that the pale gaunt waif of the sea—a sad jetsam!—had swooned upon the yellow sand, while the bright-haired lady of Ogygia had gazed in wonder upon him.

Circe had enthralled Ulysses for a year in her palace of wine and sorcery and lust. That was a time of fierce sinful pleasures, of wild deliriums.

The fire had blazed, burnt, and died away in that still marble house in the wood.

But how different these nine dreamy years! The mild-eyed, loving goddess lay in the hero's arms each night in tender love and sleep. She was no Circe, but a lady of quieter delights. Her spell was upon him, he was chained to her kind side by a magic influence, but she loved him, and was no Circe.

Nine long years!

Those old valiant mariners from the plains of Troyland were only white bones now, part of the sea-bed. They were far-off, remote, sweet sad memories.

Calypso was the slow and gracious music to which his life moved now. Often he doubted all the past. They were phantoms all those old half-forgotten people.

So he lay sleeping among the violets. The scented wind gave a myriad whispers to the poplars. The four springs sang a thin jocund song as they burst from the dark rich earth into the sunshine, and within her cave the goddess threw the golden shuttle and made a low crooning music as she thought of her stately warrior hard by, and sent him dreams of her white neck and wealth of golden hair.

She knew he would never leave her now. Her spells were too strong. Her love too great.

During the first years he had been wont to wander away to a lonely part of the shore. He would sit gazing with haunted eyes out over the sea, and his thoughts went to Penelope, and he shed a tear for old King Laertes and whispered to little Telemachus.

But that also was over for him now. Ithaca was but a misty cloud, and the dear ones there but dreams in this island of dreams.

The face of Ulysses was changed. The hard lines of endeavour, the brown painting of the wind, had gone from it. Noble and beautiful still, but even in sleep it could be seen to have lost its force.

Suddenly, in the dim recesses of the grove, there was a silence. The birds stopped singing, and the murmur of the insects droned, swelled louder, and died away.

Nothing was heard for a moment but the trickle of the streams, and then this also faded from sound.

By the side of the sleeping hero stood the tall white figure of Athene. At her feet yellow flowers broke out like little flames, and her deep, grave eyes were bent full upon Ulysses.

Perhaps he felt that unearthly majesty above him, for he turned and moaned in his sleep.

The goddess, like a statue of white marble, stood looking down at him for several moments. Then with a little sigh she stooped and touched his forehead with her long slender fingers.

The birds began a full-throated ecstasy of song, which filled the wood with a sound as of a myriad tiny flutes. The furry bees went swinging through the sunlit grove with deep organ music, the shrill tinkle of the streams sent its cool message once more into the hot swooning air.

Where the goddess had stood there was nothing but a clump of yellow crocus and some violets more vivid than the rest.

Ulysses awoke with sudden stammerings like a frightened child. He looked round him with strange troubled eyes.

Then slowly he rose up and walked through the wood towards the cave of Calypso.

Forgotten fingers were upon the latch of his brain, old scenes began to move through it in swift familiar panorama, he was as a man who wakened from a sleep of years.

One word burst from his lips—"Penelope!" His face cleared as though a mist had suddenly dispersed before it, and his walk quickened into a firm, long stride as he came out on to the lawn.

He stopped short as he saw the mouth of the cave. Calypso was pacing up and down with her sinuous graceful step, and at her side walked a tall

young man with a golden wand in his hand and winged sandals upon his feet.

And Ulysses knew him for the God Hermes who had given him the sacred herb in Circe's island and who had led him down the gloomy ways of Hades.

They turned and came towards him.

"He will never wish to go, Hermes," he heard Calypso say as they drew near.

"King," said the god, "I am come to you with a message from Father Zeus. He hath seen you lying in this island with the goddess, and bids me tell you of Ithaca and home once more, that your heart may beat strong within you and you may adventure forth and find your wife Penelope in your ancestral house. And the father promises you divine protection. Your long wanderings shall be at an end, and you shall come safely to the land of your heart's desire. Is it your will to go and leave the lady?"

The goddess laughed a little musical laugh of certain triumph.

"Go!" she cried. "Ah, he will not go, Hermes. Could he not have left me any time these nine long years of love? Go! No, my mariner loves too well the soft couches of Ogygia, and these weak arms can yet hold his wisdom captive. How will you answer, my heart's love?"

"To Ithaca?" said Ulysses.

"Yes, to Penelope thy wife, who sorroweth for thee and is in peril," answered the god.

A bright light flashed into Ulysses' eyes and his cheek was flushed with hope.

"Now have I tarried too long in this place," he cried. "I know not why, but never before has my heart burned within me as now. Yes, to Ithaca! back to my father and my wife and the old hills of home! Zeus be praised, for I who was asleep waken this day, and manhood is mine once more."

Then Calypso drooped her lovely head like a tired flower as the God Hermes flashed up into the sky like a beam of light.

"I see something of which I know not has come over you, lord of my heart," she said sadly. "I have no more power, save only the power of my deep love for you which you have forgotten. Who am I that I can combat the will of Zeus or the hardness of your heart? I have loved you well and cherished you, and shall I love you less now? No, I am no cruel goddess. Go, and my heart be with you; and what power is mine to aid you that shall you have. I doubt," she said, with a sudden burst of anger, "I doubt you have some greater goddess than I at your side, some lovelier lady, else how could my spell be broken? But now come within and make a farewell feast with me. My heart is sick and I would die. But one thing I can give you if you will not go. Would you be immortal? Stay with your lover and that gift is yours. Never shall death touch you or age. I am a goddess and can never die. Am I less beautiful than Penelope, or less kind?"

Ulysses answered her pleadings slowly and painfully.

"My queen and goddess, I know indeed that Penelope can never compare with such immortal loveliness as yours. Yes, she will grow old and wrinkled, and must die. Yet night and day all my heart must go out to her, and I would endure a thousand storms and sorrows to see home once more."

"Because of my great love for you, go, and may all the gods shower blessings on you and protect you," she said in a low voice, and her eyes were all blind with tears.

On a red evening Calypso stood alone on a rock that jutted out into the sea.

A black speck against the setting sun showed clear and far away.

Then the night fell, and she wandered weeping through her scented avenues.

But her heart was away on the moaning sea, away with Ulysses the departed.

THE LAST EPISODE

How the King came Home again after the Long Years

With the tears blinding his eyes, with shaking hands, speechless with the happy thoughts surging in his brain, Ulysses knelt and kissed the dear, dear shores of his own country.

The same rocky coasts, the same great mountain in the centre of the island raising its head into the clouds, everywhere eternally the same, and how beloved! was it not all mist and dreams—the long past? How he heard the Sirens sing, seen the swaying arms of the foul Scylla, and dwelt in love and slumber with Calypso?

And by his side once more stood the goddess, serene and beautiful in her benevolent but awful calm. From her lips he had heard that here, even here in his own land, in the fields of his inheritance, one more supreme effort awaited him. He had learnt how his palace was full of riotous princes, who wooed his wife, the Queen Penelope. He knew how his son, the goodly Prince Telemachus, was least in his own house, and how wild revel and wantonness ate up his substance. The

queen in peril! Penelope all but given up to the desires of lust and greed. All his great heart burnt with anger and hate against the suitors, and yet, with a strange dual emotion, beat high with pride for his dear and stainless lady, who still mourned for her husband, and longed against hope for his return.

He kissed the kindly home-ground, and at that sacred contact a sense of strength and power came to him, a god-like power, that in all his long toils and wanderings he had never known before.

He became conscious that Athene was speaking to him. "And remember ever, my Ulysses, that now thou hast need of all thy wit and cunning. In all the chances of thy life before never hadst thou need to walk as warily as now. For mere strength and valour unallied to wisdom and cunning will avail one nothing against the hundred. But at the hour of need I will be once more with thee if thou doest well and wisely. Courage! son of Laertes! 'tis but a little while till the end. Let not thy love and hate master thee until the appointed hour. And now, that thou mayest walk in thy palace and groves unknown for who thou art, I give thee a disguise. And so farewell until the hour of triumph."

She stretched out her spear over the kneeling king. The firm flesh dried and wrinkled upon his arms and legs. His hair shrivelled up into grey sparseness and his eyes dimmed. He wore a tattered cloak, a thing of shreds and patches, and an old beggar's staff of ilex was in his hand.

But beneath this seeming age and weakness was hidden the true hero as strong and cunning as before.

The goddess turned into light and was no more, and with slow, tottering footsteps Ulysses took a lonely way among the well-remembered paths of his native hills.

After an hour's travelling he came out on a smooth pasture land, with a little homestead nestling among a clump of trees. His heart beat eagerly within him, for if perchance after these long years farmer Eumæus still lived, here he might gain news of his palace and perhaps a friend.

Eumæus was once the steward of the estates and a very faithful servant of his master. Ulysses approached the house. In front was a large courtyard, made by a fence of oak and hawthorn boughs, and within were twelve great pens for swine.

And in the porch sat old Eumæus himself making himself a pair of sandals, hardly changed in a single feature, though perhaps his eyes were not so bright as in the old times.

Hearing footsteps, the four fierce dogs which herded the swine rushed out of the yard and leapt angrily at the newcomer. He might have fared badly, for the great beasts were lean and evil-tempered, had not the swineherd ran out to his help and drew them off with curses.

He turned to Ulysses. "Thank the gods, old fellow," he cried, "that I was near by. A little

more and you would have been torn to pieces, and then you would be in an evil plight but I a worse! Dead would you be and past caring, but I should be disgraced. Heaven knows, I have enough trouble to bear. Here's my lawful master gone in foreign parts these long years—dead as like as not—and I sit here feeding swine for them that are but little better themselves. But come in, come in, old shrew. There's a bite of food for you within, which you need I make no doubt, and then you can tell me your story, for I am a lonely man now and like a crack of talk as well as most."

The garrulous old fellow pushed him in with busy geniality and sat him down on the goatskin, which was his bed. Then he fetched what meat and wine he could furnish, and they sat down to a frugal meal.

"What, then, about this lord of yours?" said Ulysses. "I myself have wandered far these last years. Perhaps I may have met with him, and can give you news."

The swineherd chuckled.

"Nay, if you love me," he said, "none of that, my friend. Why, every dirty old man as comes along this way has some such tale to tell. And then my poor lady up in the palace—the gods save her!—she takes them in and gives them a new cloak or what not, and believes all they say until the next one comes along. No! my dear lord is dead and never shall I look upon the like of him again. By Zeus! but he was a man if you like!"

"Well, my host, we shall see in the future," said Ulysses, in so significant a tone that the swineherd was startled for a moment.

The wind had arisen and it was a black stormy night so they went to rest early, and Eumæus slept soundly till dawn. But all through the silent hours the brain of Ulysses worked like a shuttle in a loom.

At breakfast-time, while the swineherd was preparing the meal, the dogs began to bark loudly outside, but in a welcome manner, saluting one whom they knew.

Footsteps were heard crossing the yard, and a tall young man with the first down of manhood on his lip stood in the doorway.

Eumæus dropped the bowls in which he had been mixing the wine with a sudden clatter and ran towards the stranger.

"My young lord," he cried, "oh, my young lord, the sight of you is a welcome one to weary eyes. Come within my poor place. This is but a poor old man who shelters with me for a day or two. Don't mind him, my lord."

It was Telemachus the son of Ulysses.

The king rose humbly and offered his seat to his son.

"Keep your place, old man," said the prince. "The swineherd will find me another. And who may you be, and what do you in Ithaca?"

Then Ulysses told him a long story. He said that he was a Cretan, and had fought at Troy and was now destitute and a wanderer.

"Could you not take him to the palace, my lord?" said Eumæus. "Perhaps he might find some work there."

"I will clothe him, and arm him with a sword, and give him a little to help him on his way," said Telemachus, "and that most gladly. But I cannot take him to the palace. The suitors would ill-use him because of his age, perhaps they would kill him for sport. I cannot restrain them; I am young; and what is one against so many? Moreover, so great is the hate they bear towards me, they would surely slay any guest of mine."

Then Ulysses rose from his seat and bowed. "Lord," he said, "if I may dare to speak and you will hear, I say foul wrong is wrought against you in your palace, and my blood rages when I think of it."

"Old fellow, you are right enough," said the boy, sadly. "Oh, for my dead sire! to sweep these dogs from Ithaca!"

"Yes, the king!" said Eumæus, with a deep sigh.

Suddenly Ulysses saw the tall figure of Athene was standing by his side.

The other two were looking towards him, but could see nothing of her presence. The goddess looked at him with kindly eyes and touched him with her spear.

Telemachus and Eumæus crouched trembling and speechless against the furthest side of the hut.

The bronze came back to the face of the king, his hair fell from his head in all its old luxuriance,

his figure filled out, and he stood before them in his full stature and all the glory of his manhood.

Eumæus fell upon his knees and covered his eyes with his hand.

"A god! a god!" he cried, "a god has come to us! Hail, oh Immortal One, guest of my poor homestead!"

Telemachus knelt also. "Oh, Divine stranger, a boon! Tell me of my dear father, if indeed he lives and knows of the peril of his house. And will he ever come back to sit in his own chair and rule?"

Then Ulysses stepped to his son and caught him in his arms and kissed him.

"Telemachus! Telemachus!" he said, "no god am I, but your own dear father come home at last, and I am come with doom and death for the insolent ones about my board!"

And when they had all three mingled their happy tears, Telemachus said, "Father, I know how great a warrior you are, and all the world rings with the wisdom and valour of your deeds. But we two can never fight against so many. In all, the princes number a hundred and a score of men; and they are all trained fighting men, the best from Ithaca and all the neighbouring islands. We must have other aid."

"Comfort yourself, son," said Ulysses. "Aid we have, and the mightiest of all. Athene herself watches over my fortunes and will come in the hour of need. She has brought me hither and given me this disguise, and in all the coming

contest her voice will help and her arm be for us. Should we need more aid than that?"

"Truly, my father," said the boy, "we are well favoured, and my heart leaps within me at what is to come."

As he finished speaking, once more the manhood of Ulysses left him and only a poor old beggar man stood before the swineherd and the prince.

"Now will we go to the palace," said Ulysses. "I shall seem but a poor old beggar man, and however the princes may ill-use me I shall do nothing till the time has come and we are ready, and I charge you, my son, and my good friend Eumæus, that you do nothing to protect me however I am treated. You may check them by words if you can, but no more. And not even the queen herself must know that the king has come home again.

"And now let us go. The judge is set, the doom begun; none shall stay it!"

And the three went out from the hut over the mountain paths towards the palace.

The revel was at its height in the courtyard of the palace. Stone seats ran round the wall which enclosed the buildings. Over a low colonnade the orchard trees drooped into the court, and a huge vine trailed its weight of fruit over the marble.

The hot afternoon sun sent a vivid colour over everything. Beyond the palace the blue

mountains towered into a sky of deeper blue. Purple shadows from the buildings lay upon the white marble, and the long light glittered on a great table piled with golden cups and bowls, holding the *débris* of the feast.

A wild uproar and shouting filled the air.

The court was filled with whirling figures of men and girls half drunk with wine and excitement as they moved in the figures of a lascivious dance.

All the household girls were there with the suitors joining in the feast, and peals of laughter shivered through the sunny air.

Telemachus sat on a seat apart watching the revel with keen eyes. There was a repressed excitement in his face and an eager regard. One of the girls noticed it as she strolled past. She was a slight, fair wanton creature with a mocking smile.

"How, Lord Telemachus?" she said, laughing lightly, "are you not going to join us in the fun? You make a sorry host indeed! Is not this your palace, and do you leave us without your countenance. Oh, shame upon you for a laggard youth when wine and kisses wait you."

She made an impudent grimace at him and flitted past. But a short time back he would have raged at this impudent salutation from a pretty slave girl who drew a confident strength from the protection of his enemies. But now he hardly heard her, but leant forward again in the attitude of one who watches and waits.

Outside the palace gate, on the hot white road, two old men were approaching. One was the swineherd Eumæus and the other a wandering beggar man.

Just by the threshold of the courtyard an old lean dog, very grey and feeble, lay upon a heap of dung in the sunlight. The mailed horse-flies hovered round him in swarms, but he seemed too weak to drive them away. As the beggar approached he threw his muzzle up into the air with a quick movement. His sightless eyes turned towards the advancing footsteps. With a great effort he scrambled to his feet. The lean tail wagged in tremulous joy, the scarred ears were pricked in welcome.

He stumbled to the feet of Ulysses. When he touched him the old dog lay down in the dust and with a long sigh he died.

And this was the first welcome the king had to his palace, and as he went in through the gates his eyes were wet with tears.

When Telemachus saw the steward he beckoned him to the table and sat beside him while he ate. But Ulysses crouched down by the threshold. Telemachus gave bread and meat to the swineherd.

"Go, Eumæus," he said aloud, "give these broken meats to that poor old beggar man by the gate, and tell him from me that if he lacks he should be bold and go to the princes and ask them for alms. By Zeus! he will never grow fat if he crouches by the door there!"

Ulysses took the food with a low bow and packed it away in his wallet.

He rose up grasping his staff, and went tottering among the suitors. His lean arms and furrowed, wrinkled face were so piteous, his whining appeal full of such misery, that many of the princes tossed him something.

At the head of the table a tall and splendid young man was sitting. He was richly dressed in a showy, ostentatious manner. His florid, handsome face wore a perpetual and evil sneer. His grey eyes were ill-tempered and quarrelsome.

"By the gods, my friends," he cried, with a sneer, "how tender-hearted and compassionate you are grown! With what lavishness do you bestow the wealth of Ulysses, or rather of the queen, upon this old scarecrow. Such old beasts are no use in this world. Get you gone, you old dog!"

With that he hurled a three-legged stool at Ulysses. The stool struck him a heavy blow on his side.

For a moment the black turmoil in the hero's heart was almost irrepressible. But with an enormous effort of will he overcame it. He stood quite still, with his head sunk upon his breast in humility.

Now came the girls from out of the house carrying great jars of fresh wine, and copper bowls of water for the mixing, which they put upon the table.

Here was better sport than an old beggar and his woes, and Ulysses moved aside and was forgotten.

But one of the girls touched him on the shoulder. "Wanderer," said she, "the Queen Penelope has seen how Antinous used you from her room within the hall, and she sends me to summon you to her, for she would speak to you."

Then, with beating heart and footsteps which trembled with no simulated age, the king followed the girl over the threshold of his own palace.

As he was walking towards the chamber of the queen an old woman came towards them, a very old woman with a lined brown face and little, brilliant twinkling eyes.

"Poor old man," she said, "it is a shame that they should use your grey hairs so, and abuse the hospitality which is the sacred right of strangers. My lady Penelope sends me to you, and bids me wash your feet in this bowl of water, so that we may purge our house of the stain the prince without has cast upon it. Sit on this stool and I will lave ye."

So the old nurse Euryclea bathed the feet of her master whom she had dandled in her arms as a child. Suddenly Ulysses made as though he would draw away his foot. He remembered that on his leg he bore a strange-shaped scar made by a savage boar when he was a boy, and he feared the wise old woman would know him by that mark.

But as she passed her hand along his ankle she touched the mark and turned his foot towards the light and saw it. She dropped his foot quickly, and the basin was overturned and the water ran

away over the marble floor. She looked up into the king's face and knew him for all his disguise.

In a fierce, hurried whisper he bade her be silent for her life and his and the queen's safety. As she vowed, trembling, by Zeus and the gods, to do his bidding, a trumpet snarled suddenly outside on the steps of the palace.

The riot without died into silence.

The clear cold voice of a herald began to speak.

Thus says the Queen Penelope: "To-morrow will I make an end of all. In the forenoon I will choose from among the princes whom I will wed. Too long have ye rioted within the palace and eaten up the substance of myself and my son. I am aweary. And since there is no other way, to-morrow I will choose. Ye shall take the great bow of the King Ulysses from its cover. And he who can shoot an arrow through twelve axes in a row—even as Ulysses was wont to do—him will I wed."

"Nurse!" whispered Ulysses, "the king will be here before any can bend that bow. Now go into the queen and tell her that the old man is sick and begs leave to wait upon her another time. And comfort her with an omen that you have seen, but tell her nothing. And now farewell. There is much to do ere dawn."

There was a silence of consternation in the great banqueting hall of the palace.

Penelope from her seat upon the raised steps

beneath the richly-decorated wall at the end smiled faintly to herself.

The twelve axes stood in a row, driven into sockets in the pavement. The suitors stood in two long rows on either side.

Antinous, the strongest of them all, held a great polished bow. His face blazed with anger and was red with shame.

All eyes were centred on him. No one saw old Eumæus steal out into the porch and silently lower the heavy bars of the door and lash them tight with cords.

"Ah!" cried Antinous, "I know now why neither any of you nor I myself can bend this bow. It is not the great strength of Ulysses, for I am stronger than he ever was. This is Apollo's festival, the Archer-God, and it is useless to strive to bend this bow to-day. Let us sacrifice to Helios to-day, and then to-morrow come again to the trial."

Then the old beggar man came forward.

"My lords," he said, "I pray you give me the bow, since you have done your trial for to-day. I was once strong in my youth. Let me have this honour."

Antinous scowled at him, and stepped toward him to strike such insolence, but the clear voice of Penelope called sharply down the lane of men,—

"Who insults even the meanest in my palace? Have more regard, sir, for I am still queen here. Give the old man the bow since that is his whim."

Antinous was cowed, but still murmured, when

Telemachus stepped quickly up to him. The boy seemed taller, his eyes shone with a cold, fierce light they had never seen in them before. His voice rang with a new authority.

"Be silent, sir!" he said in a keen, threatening voice. "The bow is mine, and mine alone, to give or refuse as I decide. Mother, the trial is over for to-day. Go with your maidens into your own chamber. I will see to this old man, and I am master here and will be so."

With a frightened pride and wonder the queen withdrew.

The suitors began to whisper to each other, wondering what this might mean. Their confidence seemed to be slipping away from them. Each and all felt uneasy. There was some strange influence in the air which sapped their courage and silenced the loud insolent words which were ever on their lips.

The shadow of death was creeping into the hall.

The great marble room suddenly grew cold. The old beggar came up to the splendid Antinous and took the bow from his unresisting hand.

As he plucked the string the gods spake at last. A crash of thunder pealed among them. There was a moment's silence, and then the bow-string rang beneath the hero's touch as clear as the note of a swallow.

And in a strange light, which glowed out from the walls and great pillars of bronze, the princes saw no beggar, but a noble form with bronzed face and flashing eyes, and they knew the king had come home again.

Ulysses motioned to his son, and Telemachus drew his sword and with a great shout rushed up the hall after his father.

They turned and stood on the steps.

An arrow sang like a flying wasp, and Antinous lay dying on the floor.

Then the princes rushed to the walls where their armour and swords were wont to hang, but all the pegs were bare.

Only above the steps where Ulysses stood were three spears and three shields, and as they gazed in cold fear Eumæus leapt upon the steps and the three girded on the armour.

Again the great bow sang, and Amphinomus lay dead.

Then Telemachus with a great shout drove his spear through the fat Ctessipus, and he fell gurgling his life away.

But one of the suitors, Melanthius, climbed up a pillar through one of the lanterns of the hall and clambered over the roofs to the armoury unseen by Ulysses.

And while the deadly arrows sped with bitter mocking words towards the cowering throng, he gathered a great sheaf of spears and flung them down among his comrades.

They seized upon the spears with a fierce cry of joy, and Ulysses' heart failed him where he stood for there were still many living.

They began to run up the hall towards the steps.

Then at last Athene saw that her time had come, and she lifted her terrible war shield which brings death to the sons of men.

And the flight of spears all went far wide of the mark, and some fell with a rattle upon the floor.

With one cry of triumph the king leapt like light among the crowd. Hither and there flashed the three swords like swooping vultures, and Athene took all power from the princes, and one by one they screamed and met their doom.

And soon the din of battle died away, and save for a faint moaning the hall was silent.

And the princes, the pride of the islands, lay fallen in dust and blood, heaped one on the other, like a great catch of fishes turned out from a fisherman's nets upon the shore.

Eumæus went to the door of the hall and cut the lashings, and raised the bars so that the sunlight came slanting in great beams. The dust danced in the light rays like a powder of tiny lives.

Then Ulysses called the servants and bade them carry the bodies away. And he ordered Euryclea to wash the blood-stained floors, and to bring sulphur and torches that the place might be purified.

And that night great beacons flared on the hills, and far out to sea the fishermen saw them and said, "Surely the king has come home again."

And while the music rang though the lighted palace and the people passed before the gates

shouting for joy, old Euryclea spread the marriage bed of the king by the light of flaming torches.

And when all was prepared, the old nurse went to Ulysses and Penelope and led them to the door of the marriage chamber, as she had led them twenty years before.

Then the music ceased in the palace halls and silence fell over all the house.